Piggiawiggia Pyramidalis

To Sue, with thanks

J.N.

Published by Dial Books for Young Readers
A Division of Penguin Books USA Inc.
375 Hudson Street
New York, New York 10014

First published by Aurum Books for Children, London
Copyright © 1990 by Aurum Books for Children
Illustrations © 1990 by Jill Newton
Printed and bound in Italy by LEGO
E
1 3 5 7 9 10 8 6 4 2

Library of Congress Cataloging in Publication Data
Lear, Edward, 1812-1888.
Of pelicans and pussycats / by Edward Lear;
pictures by Jill Newton.
p. cm.
Summary: A selection of poems and limericks by Edward Lear,
including "The Quangle Wangle's Hat," "The Pelican Chorus,"
and "The Courtship of the Yonghy-Bonghy-Bò."
ISBN 0-8037-0728-2
1. Children's poetry, English.
[1. Nonsense verses. 2.Limericks. 3. English poetry.]
1. Newton, Jill, 1964 – ill. II. Title.
PR4879.L2A6 1990   821'.8—dc20   89-37618   CIP   AC

The full-color artwork was prepared with ink and watercolors.
It was then color-separated and reproduced as red, blue, yellow,
and black halftones.

Of Pelicans and Pussycats

POEMS AND LIMERICKS

by **Edward Lear**
pictures by **Jill Newton**

DIAL BOOKS
FOR YOUNG READERS
New York

The Quangle Wangle's Hat

On top of the Crumpetty Tree
The Quangle Wangle sat,
But his face you could not see,
On account of his Beaver Hat.
For his Hat was a hundred and two feet wide,
With ribbons and bibbons on every side
And bells, and buttons, and loops, and lace,
So that nobody ever could see the face
Of the Quangle Wangle Quee.

The Quangle Wangle said
To himself on the Crumpetty Tree,
"Jam and jelly and bread
Are the best food for me!
But the longer I live on this Crumpetty Tree
The plainer than ever it seems to me
That very few people come this way
And that life on the whole is far from gay!"
Said the Quangle Wangle Quee.

But there came to the Crumpetty Tree,
Mr. and Mrs. Canary;
And they said, "Did you ever see
Any spot so charmingly airy?
May we build a nest on your lovely Hat?
Mr. Quangle Wangle, grant us that!
O please let us come and build a nest
Of whatever material suits you best,
Mr. Quangle Wangle Quee!"

And besides, to the Crumpetty Tree
Came the Stork, the Duck, and the Owl;
The Snail, and the Bumble-Bee,
The Frog, and the Fimble Fowl;
(The Fimble Fowl, with a Corkscrew leg;)
And all of them said, "We humbly beg,
We may build our homes on your lovely Hat,
Mr. Quangle Wangle, grant us that!
Mr. Quangle Wangle Quee!"

And the Golden Grouse came there,
And the Pobble who has no toes,
And the small Olympian bear,
And the Dong with a luminous nose.
And the Blue Baboon, who played the flute,
And the Orient Calf from the Land of Tute,
And the Attery Squash, and the Bisky Bat,
All came and built on the lovely Hat
Of the Quangle Wangle Quee.

And the Quangle Wangle said
To himself on the Crumpetty Tree,
"When all these creatures move
What a wonderful noise there'll be!"
And at night by the light of the Mulberry moon
They danced to the flute of the Blue Baboon,
On the broad green leaves of the Crumpetty Tree,
And all were as happy as happy could be,
With the Quangle Wangle Quee.

There was an Old Person of Bree,
     Who frequented the depths of the sea;
She nurs'd the small fishes, and washed all the dishes,
     And swam back again into Bree.

There was an Old Person of Ware,
     Who rode on the back of a bear;
When they ask'd, "Does it trot?" he said, "Certainly not!
     He's a Moppsikon Floppsikon bear!"

The Owl and the Pussycat

The Owl and the Pussycat went to sea
In a beautiful pea-green boat,
They took some honey, and plenty of money,
Wrapped up in a five-pound note.
The Owl looked up to the stars above,
And sang to a small guitar,
"O lovely Pussy! O Pussy, my love,
What a beautiful Pussy you are,
You are,
You are!
What a beautiful Pussy you are!"

Pussy said to the Owl, "You elegant fowl!
How charmingly sweet you sing!
O let us be married! Too long we have tarried:
But what shall we do for a ring?"
They sailed away, for a year and a day,
To the land where the Bong-tree grows,
And there in a wood a Piggy-wig stood
With a ring at the end of his nose,
His nose,
His nose,
With a ring at the end of his nose.

"Dear Pig, are you willing to sell for one shilling
Your ring?" Said the Piggy, "I will."
So they took it away, and were married next day
By the Turkey who lives on the hill.
They dined on mince, and slices of quince,
Which they ate with a runcible spoon;
And hand in hand, on the edge of the sand,
They danced by the light of the moon,
The moon,
The moon,
They danced by the light of the moon.

There was an Old Man of Dumbree,
   Who taught little owls to drink tea;
For he said, "To eat mice, is not proper or nice,"
   That amiable man of Dumbree.

There was an Old Man who said, "How
   Shall I flee from this horrible Cow?
I will sit on this stile, and continue to smile,
   Which may soften the heart of that Cow."

The Pelican Chorus

King and Queen of the Pelicans we;
No other Birds so grand we see!
None but we have feet like fins!
With lovely leathery throats and chins!
Ploffskin, Pluffskin, Pelican jee!
We think no Birds so happy as we!
Plumpskin, Ploshkin, Pelican jill!
We think so then, and we thought so still!

We live on the Nile. The Nile we love.
By night we sleep on the cliffs above;
By day we fish, and at eve we stand
On long bare islands of yellow sand.
And when the sun sinks slowly down
And the great rock walls grow dark and brown,
Where the purple river rolls fast and dim
And the Ivory Ibis starlike skim,
Wing to wing we dance around,
Stamping our feet with a flumpy sound,
Opening our mouths as Pelicans ought,
And this is the song we nightly snort:
Ploffskin, Pluffskin, Pelican jee,
We think no Birds so happy as we!
Plumpskin, Ploshkin, Pelican jill,
We think so then, and we thought so still.

Last year came out our Daughter, Dell;
And all the Birds received her well.
To do her honor, a feast we made
For every bird that can swim or wade.
Herons and Gulls, and Cormorants black,
Cranes, and Flamingoes with scarlet back,
Plovers and Storks, and Geese in clouds,
Swans and Dilberry Ducks in crowds.
Thousands of Birds in wondrous flight!
They ate and drank and danced all night,
And echoing back from the rocks you heard
Multitude-echoes from Bird and Bird,
Ploffskin, Pluffskin, Pelican jee,
We think no Birds so happy as we!
Plumpskin, Ploshkin, Pelican jill,
We think so then, and we thought so still!

Yes, they came; and among the rest,
The King of the Cranes all grandly dressed.
Such a lovely tail! Its feathers float
Between the ends of his blue dress coat;
With pea-green trousers all so neat,
And a delicate frill to hide his feet,
(For though no one speaks of it, everyone knows,
He has got no webs between his toes!)

As soon as he saw our Daughter, Dell,
In violent love that Crane King fell,
On seeing her waddling form so fair,
With a wreath of shrimps in her short white hair.
And before the end of the next long day,
Our Dell had given her heart away;
For the King of the Cranes had won that heart,
With a Crocodile's egg and a large fishtart.
She vowed to marry the King of the Cranes,
Leaving the Nile for stranger plains;
And away they flew in a gathering crowd
Of endless birds in a lengthening cloud.
Ploffskin, Pluffskin, Pelican jee,
We think no Birds so happy as we!
Plumpskin, Ploshkin, Pelican jill,
We think so then, and we thought so still!

And far away in the twilight sky,
We heard them singing a lessening cry,
Farther and farther till out of sight,
And we stood alone in the silent night!
Often since, in the nights of June,
We sit on the sand and watch the moon;
She has gone to the great Gromboolian plain,
And we probably never shall meet again!
Oft, in the long still nights of June,
We sit on the rocks and watch the moon;
She dwells by the streams of the Chankly Bore,
And we probably never shall see her more.
Ploffskin, Pluffskin, Pelican jee,
We think no Birds so happy as we!
Plumpskin, Ploshkin, Pelican jill,
We think so then, and we thought so still!

The Pelican Chorus

The Yonghy-Bonghy-Bò

The Courtship of the Yonghy-Bonghy-Bò

On the Coast of Coromandel
Where the early pumpkins blow,
In the middle of the woods
Lived the Yonghy-Bonghy-Bò.
Two old chairs, and half a candle,
One old jug without a handle,
These were all his worldly goods:
In the middle of the woods,
These were all the worldly goods,
Of the Yonghy-Bonghy-Bò,
Of the Yonghy-Bonghy-Bò.

Once, among the Bong-trees walking
Where the early pumpkins blow,
To a little heap of stones
Came the Yonghy-Bonghy-Bò.
There he heard a Lady talking,
To some milk-white Hens of Dorking,
"'Tis the Lady Jingly Jones!
On that little heap of stones
Sits the Lady Jingly Jones!"
Said the Yonghy-Bonghy-Bò,
Said the Yonghy-Bonghy-Bò.

"Lady Jingly! Lady Jingly!
Sitting where the pumpkins blow,
Will you come and be my wife?"
Said the Yonghy-Bonghy-Bò.
"I am tired of living singly,
On this coast so wild and shingly,
I'm a-weary of my life:
If you'll come and be my wife,
Quite serene would be my life!"
Said the Yonghy-Bonghy-Bò,
Said the Yonghy-Bonghy-Bò.

"On this Coast of Coromandel,
Shrimps and watercresses grow,
Prawns are plentiful and cheap,"
Said the Yonghy-Bonghy-Bò.
"You shall have my chairs and candle,
And my jug without a handle!
Gaze upon the rolling deep
(Fish is plentiful and cheap)
As the sea, my love is deep!"
Said the Yonghy-Bonghy-Bò,
Said the Yonghy-Bonghy-Bò.

Lady Jingly answered sadly,
And her tears began to flow,
"Your proposal comes too late,
Mr. Yonghy-Bonghy-Bò!
I would be your wife most gladly!"
(Here she twirled her fingers madly,)
"But in England I've a mate!
Yes! you've asked me far too late,
For in England I've a mate,
Mr. Yonghy-Bonghy-Bò!
Mr. Yonghy-Bonghy-Bò!"

"Mr. Jones (his name is Handel,
Handel Jones, Esquire, & Co.)
Dorking fowls delights to send,
Mr. Yonghy-Bonghy-Bò!
Keep, oh! keep your chairs and candle,
And your jug without a handle,
I can merely be your friend!
Should my Jones more Dorkings send,
I will give you three, my friend!
Mr. Yonghy-Bonghy-Bò!
Mr. Yonghy-Bonghy-Bò!"

"Though you've such a tiny body,
And your head so large doth grow,
Though your hat may blow away,
Mr. Yonghy-Bonghy-Bò!
Though you're such a Hoddy Doddy
Yet I wish that I could modi-
fy the words I needs must say!
Will you please to go away?
That is all I have to say
Mr. Yonghy-Bonghy-Bò!
Mr. Yonghy-Bonghy-Bò!"

Down the slippery slopes of Myrtle,
Where the early pumpkins blow,
To the calm and silent sea
Fled the Yonghy-Bonghy-Bò.
There, beyond the Bay of Gurtle,
Lay a large and lively Turtle;
"You're the Cove," he said, "for me,
On your back beyond the sea,
Turtle, you shall carry me!"
Said the Yonghy-Bonghy-Bò,
Said the Yonghy-Bonghy-Bò.

Through the silent-roaring ocean
Did the Turtle swiftly go;
Holding fast upon his shell
Rode the Yonghy-Bonghy-Bò.
With a sad primeval motion
Toward the sunset isles of Boshen
Still the Turtle bore him well.
Holding fast upon his shell,
"Lady Jingly Jones, farewell!"
Sang the Yonghy-Bonghy-Bò,
Sang the Yonghy-Bonghy-Bò.

From the Coast of Coromandel,
Did that Lady never go;
On that heap of stones she mourns
For the Yonghy-Bonghy-Bò.
On that Coast of Coromandel,
In his jug without a handle
Still she weeps, and daily moans;
On that little heap of stones
To her Dorking Hens she moans,
For the Yonghy-Bonghy-Bò,
For the Yonghy-Bonghy-Bò.

There was an Old Man of Dundee,
Who frequented the top of a tree;
When disturbed by the crows, he abruptly arose,
And exclaimed, "I'll return to Dundee."

There was an Old Man with a beard,
Who said, "It is just as I feared!
Two Owls and a Hen, four Larks and a Wren,
Have all built their nests in my beard!"

The Table and the Chair

Said the Table to the Chair,
"You can hardly be aware,
How I suffer from the heat,
And the chilblains on my feet!
If we took a little walk,
We might have a little talk!
Pray let us take the air!"
Said the Table to the Chair.

Said the Chair unto the Table,
"Now you know we are not able!
How foolishly you talk,
When you know we cannot walk!"
Said the Table, with a sigh,
"It can do no harm to try,
I've as many legs as you,
Why can't we walk on two?"

So they both went slowly down,
And walked about the town
With a cheerful bumpy sound,
As they toddled round and round.
And everybody cried,
As they hastened to their side,
"See! the Table and the Chair
Have come out to take the air!"

But in going down an alley,
To a castle in a valley,
They completely lost their way,
And wandered all the day,
Till, to see them safely back,
They paid a Ducky-quack,
And a Beetle, and a Mouse,
Who took them to their house.

Then they whispered to each other,
"O delightful little brother!
What a lovely walk we've taken!
Let us dine on Beans and Bacon!"
So the Ducky, and the leetle
Browny-Mousy and the Beetle
Dined, and danced upon their heads
Till they toddled to their beds.

The New Vestments

There lived an old man in the Kingdom of Tess,
Who invented a purely original dress;
And when it was perfectly made and complete,
He opened the door, and walked into the street.

By way of a Hat, he'd a loaf of Brown Bread,
In the middle of which he inserted his head;
His Shirt was made up of no end of dead Mice,
The warmth of whose skins was quite fluffy and nice;
His Drawers were of Rabbit skins; so were his Shoes;
His Stockings were skins, but it is not known whose;
His Waistcoat and Trousers were made of Pork Chops;
His Buttons were Jujubes, and Chocolate Drops;
His Coat was all Pancakes with Jam for a border,
And a girdle of Biscuits to keep it in order;
And he wore over all, as a screen from bad weather,
A Cloak of green Cabbage-leaves stitched all together.

He had walked a short way, when he heard a great noise,
Of all sorts of Beasticles, Birdlings, and Boys;

And from every long street and dark lane in the town
Beasts, Birdles, and Boys in a tumult rushed down.
Two Cows and a half ate his Cabbage-leaf Cloak;
Four Apes seized his Girdle, which vanished like smoke;
Three Kids ate up half of his Pancaky Coat,
And the tails were devour'd by an ancient He Goat;
An army of Dogs in a twinkling tore up his
Pork Waistcoat and Trousers to give to their Puppies;
And while they were growling, and mumbling the Chops,
Ten Boys stole the Jujubes and Chocolate Drops.

He tried to run back to his house, but in vain,
For Scores of fat Pigs came again and again;
They rushed out of stables and hovels and doors,
They tore off his stockings, his shoes, and his drawers;
And now from the housetops with screechings descend,
Striped, spotted, white, black, and gray Cats without end,
They jumped on his shoulders and knocked off his Hat,
When Crows, Ducks, and Hens made a mincemeat of that;
They speedily flew at his sleeves in a trice,
And utterly tore up his Shirt of dead Mice;
They swallowed the last of his Shirt with a squall,
Whereon he ran home with no clothes on at all.

And he said to himself as he bolted the door,
"I will not wear a similar dress any more,
Any more, any more, any more, never more!"

The Dong with a Luminous Nose

When awful darkness and silence reign
　Over the great Gromboolian plain,
　　Through the long, long wintry nights;
　　　When the angry breakers roar
　　　　As they beat on the rocky shore;
　　　　　When the Storm-clouds brood on the towering heights
　　　　　　Of the Hills of the Chankly Bore:

　　　　　　Then, through the vast and gloomy dark,
　　　　　There moves what seems a fiery spark,
　　　　A lonely spark with silvery rays
　　　Piercing the coal-black night,
　　A Meteor strange and bright:
Hither and thither the vision strays,
A single lurid light.

Slowly it wanders, pauses, creeps,
　Anon it sparkles, flashes and leaps;
　　And ever as onward it gleaming goes
　　　A light on the Bong-tree stems it throws.
　　　　And those who watch at that midnight hour
　　　　　From Hall or Terrace, or lofty Tower,
　　　　　Cry, as the wild light passes along,
　　　　　　"The Dong! the Dong!
　　　　　　　The wandering Dong through the forest goes!
　　　　　　　The Dong! the Dong!
　　　　　　　　The Dong with a luminous Nose!"

Long years ago
The Dong was happy and gay,
Till he fell in love with a Jumbly Girl
Who came to those shores one day.
For the Jumblies came in a sieve, they did,
Landing at eve near the Zemmery Fidd
Where the Oblong Oysters grow,
And the rocks are smooth and gray.
And all the woods and the valleys rang
With the Chorus they daily and nightly sang,

1 "Far and few, far and few,
Are the lands where the Jumblies live;
Their heads are green, and their hands are blue
And they went to sea in a sieve."

Happily, happily passed those days!
While the cheerful Jumblies stayed;
They danced in circlets all night long,
To the plaintive pipe of the lively Dong,
In moonlight, shine, or shade.
For day and night he was always there
By the side of the Jumbly Girl so fair,
With her sky-blue hands, and her sea-green hair.
Till the morning came of that hateful day
When the Jumblies sailed in their sieve away,
And the Dong was left on the cruel shore
Gazing-gazing for evermore,
Ever keeping his weary eyes on
That pea-green sail on the far horizon,
Singing the Jumbly Chorus still
As he sat all day on the grassy hill,

(Repeat chorus from 1)

But when the sun was low in the West,
The Dong arose and said,
"What little sense I once possessed
Has gone quite out of my head!"
And since that day he wanders still
By lake and forest, marsh and hill,
Singing, "O somewhere, in valley or plain
Might I find my Jumbly Girl again!
For ever I'll seek by lake and shore
Till I find my Jumbly Girl once more!"

Playing a pipe with silvery squeaks,
Since then his Jumbly Girl he seeks,
And because by night he could not see,
He gathered the bark of the Twangum Tree
On the flowery plain that grows.
And he wove him a wondrous Nose,
A Nose as strange as a Nose could be!
Of vast proportions and painted red,
And tied with cords to the back of his head.
In a hollow rounded space it ended
With a luminous Lamp within suspended,
All fenced about
With a bandage stout
To prevent the wind from blowing it out;
And with holes all around to send the light,
In gleaming rays on the dismal night.

And now each night, and all night long,
Over those plains still roams the Dong;
And above the wail of the Chimp and Snipe
You may hear the squeak of his plaintive pipe
While ever he seeks, but seeks in vain
To meet with his Jumbly Girl again;
Lonely and wild – all night he goes,
The Dong with a luminous Nose!
And all who watch at the midnight hour,
From Hall or Terrace, or lofty Tower,
Cry, as they trace the Meteor bright,
Moving along through the dreary night,
"This is the hour when forth he goes,
The Dong with a luminous Nose!
Yonder – over the plain he goes;
He goes!
He goes;
The Dong with a luminous Nose!"

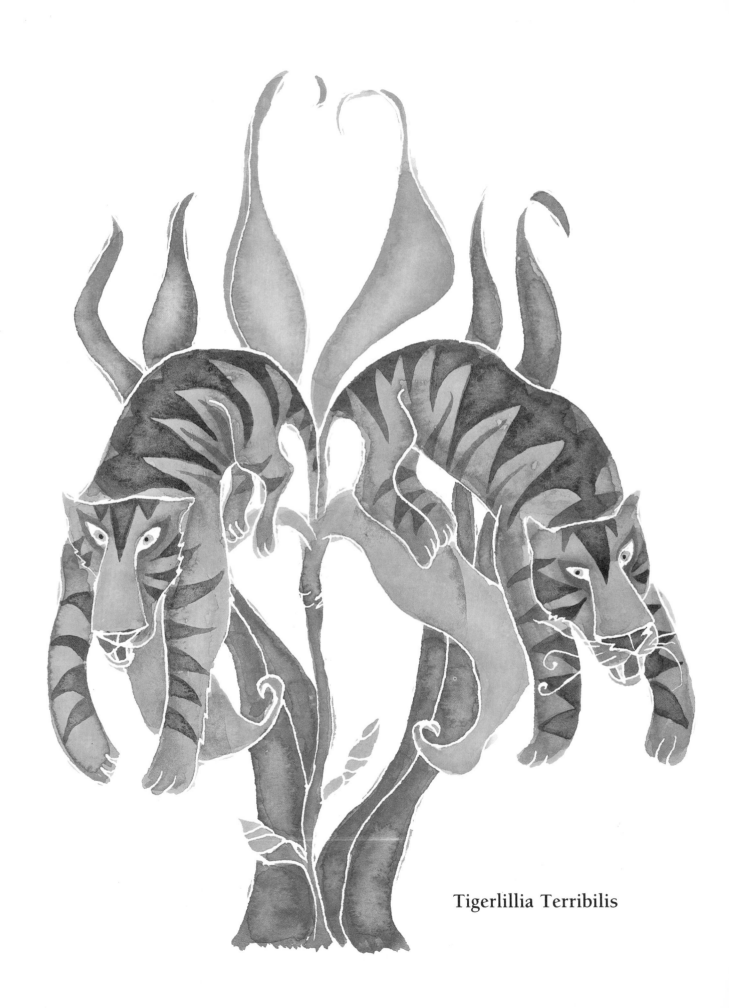

Tigerlillia Terribilis